Where Does the Man In The Moon Go During the Day?

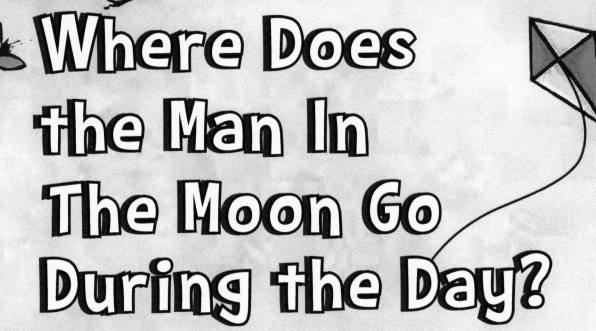

Written & Illustrated by

Jared Jackson

PAGE PUBLISHING, INC.
New York, NY

First originally published by Page Publishing, Inc. 2018

ISBN 978-1-64214-397-3 (Hardcover)
ISBN 978-1-64214-396-6 (Digital)

Printed in the United States of America

Dedication

To Arden, Ivy, Cooper, and Ruby—my
nieces and nephew who I love and adore.

While Mr. Sun fills the
sky with his light,

where does the
Man In The Moon go all day?

Does he watch television, read stories, or write,

or go to the seashore
to fly a big kite?

Is he playing a tricky, but fun-filled
board game, or checking his
mailbox to see if mail came?

Is he out on the basketball court, shooting hoops like three-pointers and dunks, or some cool alley-*OOPS*?

Is he riding the rails on a long, heavy train, or splashing and dancing around in the rain?

Is he rolling around in the crisp
leaves of fall, or meeting his
friends for a game of football?

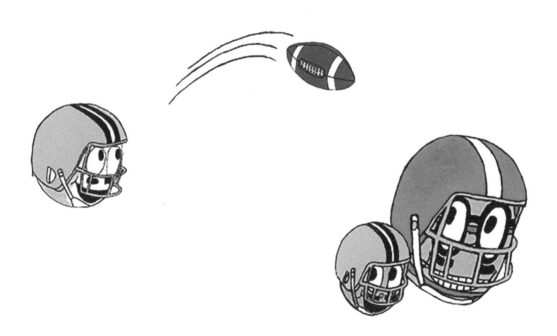

Is he driving around in a little sports car with his beautiful date who's a big movie star?

Is he twirling and spinning a big
Hula-Hoop, or singing NepTunes
in a cool music group?

Does he go to the park to play
fetch with his dog, or put on a
sweatband to go for a jog?

Does he like to relax in a hot bubble bath,
or trek through the jungle, exploring a path?

Does he put dirty clothes in the washing machine with a little detergent to get them all clean?

Maybe the jolly, round Man In
The Moon might spend his time
off as a hot-air balloon!

Is he eating a meal of a thick,
juicy steak with some corn on the
cob and a big slice of cake?

Does he
like to go
roll down a
steep, grassy hill,
or might he be sick in
bed, feeling quite ill?

Is he flying an airplane,
or surfing the tide,

or having a blast
on a carnival ride?

Could he be in his backyard, just mowing the grass, or out in a boat, catching catfish and bass?

Could he be jumping ramps on an awesome skateboard, or in the stands, cheering because his team scored?

Is he baking some cookies with little Pluto, or leading a car race with five laps to go?

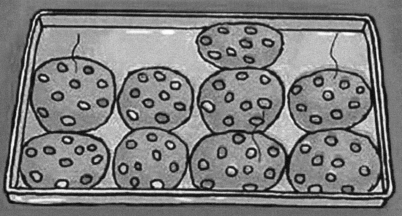

MARTIANSVILLE

22

Has he saved up his pennies, dimes, quarters, and nickels to treat his space buddies to fruity popsicles? Is he riding a horse in a wild rodeo?

Where does the Man In The Moon *really* go?

While the bright, glowing sun
fills the sky with great light,
the moon isn't easily seen

from the morning sunrise 'til
the evening sunset and all
other times in between.

26

There are beautiful blue skies, and fluffy white clouds that disguise the moon during the day. And the Man In The Moon spins around his friend, Earth,

reaching places so far, far away.

So the next time you see Moon, please, tell him "Good night," and know he'll be coming back soon. And that's only some of the outer space fun with our good friend, the Man In The Moon.

The End

About the Author

Jared grew up as the youngest of four children on his family's farm in Kentucky before moving to Tennessee after graduating from college. Though born with normal vision, he was left almost totally blind at the age of nine due to an unsuccessful surgery to remove a brain tumor. He found an interest in children's literature after writing the first version of this book for a high school English assignment. Utilizing what limited vision remains in only one eye, the treasured memories of a little boy's world before losing his sight, and his God-given talent for easily explaining how things work, Jared creates a story with his own illustrations of what might be seen through the eyes of a child.

CPSIA information can be obtained
at www.ICGtesting.com
Printed in the USA
LVHW051023240219
608524LV00002BA/2/P